DIEGO'S BABY POLAR BEAR Rescue

adapted by Lara Bergen

based on the teleplay by Chris Gifford

illustrated by Warner McGee

Ready-to-Read

Simon Spotlight/Nickelodeon

New York   London   Toronto   Sydney

Based on the TV series *Go, Diego, Go!*™ as seen on Nick Jr.®

SIMON SPOTLIGHT
An imprint of Simon & Schuster Children's Publishing Division
1230 Avenue of the Americas, New York, New York 10020
© 2009 Viacom International Inc. All rights reserved.
NICK JR., *Go, Diego, Go!*, and all related titles, logos, and characters are trademarks of Viacom International Inc.
All rights reserved, including the right of reproduction in whole or in part in any form.
SIMON SPOTLIGHT, READY-TO-READ, and colophon are registered trademarks of Simon & Schuster, Inc.
For information about special discounts for bulk purchases, please contact Simon & Schuster Special Sales at
1-866-506-1949 or business@simonandschuster.com.
Manufactured in the United States of America
First Edition
2 4 6 8 10 9 7 5 3 1
Library of Congress Cataloging-in-Publication Data
Bergen, Lara.
Diego's baby polar bear rescue / adapted by Lara Bergen. — 1st ed.
p. cm. — (Ready-to-read)
"Based on the TV series Go, Diego, Go! as seen on Nick Jr."—Copyright p.
ISBN: 978-1-4169-8495-5
I. Go, Diego, go! (Television program) II. Title.
PZ7.B44985Dik 2009
[E]—dc22
2008054529

Hi! I am 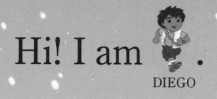.
DIEGO

I am in the Arctic,

near the top of the !
WORLD

Lots of  live in the

POLAR BEARS

Arctic.

 love to slide in the

POLAR BEARS   SNOW

and swim in the icy cold ⬤.

OCEAN

These  are swimming
POLAR BEARS

out to the .
ICE

The is where fish for
ICE   POLAR BEARS

their food.

Look! There is a in

POLAR BEAR

trouble!

She cannot swim all the way

to the 🧊.

ICE

 can help us save her.

RESCUE PACK

Can a 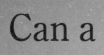 help us

SKATEBOARD

save the ?

POLAR BEAR

No.

Can a help us

JET SKI

save the ?

POLAR BEAR

Yes!

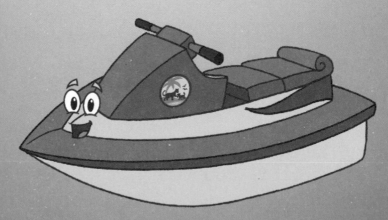

Yay! We saved the
POLAR BEAR
!

She was trying to find food for her babies.

They are on an ⬤ far away.
ISLAND

The  melted and she could not swim all the way back.

Don't worry, Mommy .

POLAR BEAR

We will bring your babies to you.

 can help us find the baby

CLICK

POLAR BEARS.

Just say ""!

CLICK

will zoom through the Arctic

CLICK

to look for the baby **.**

POLAR BEARS

Are these the baby  ?

POLAR BEARS

No, these are .

ARCTIC FOXES

Are these the baby  ?

POLAR BEARS

Yes!

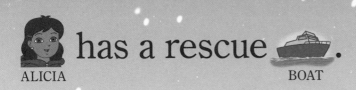 **has a rescue** 🚤**.**

ALICIA   BOAT

She can take us to the baby

POLAR BEARS **.**

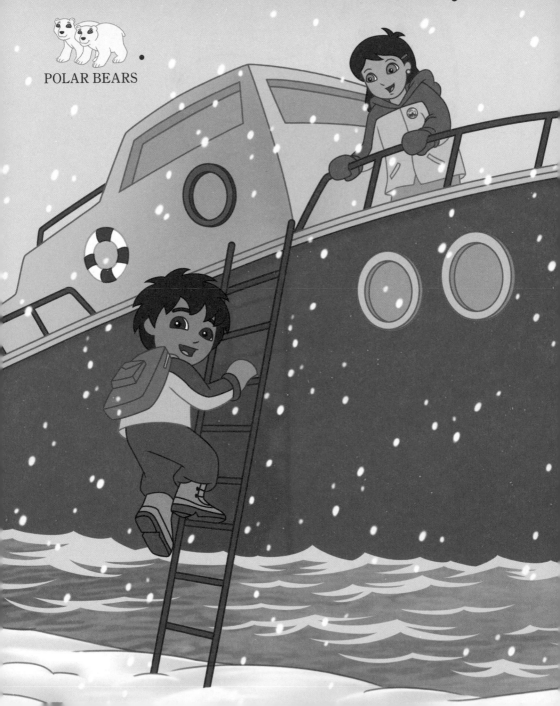

But look!

Our is too big
BOAT

to get to the 🏝️.
ISLAND

We need to find an animal

to give us a ride.

There is a .
BELUGA WHALE

Can the give us a ride?
BELUGA WHALE

Yes!

Now the are blocking our way.

WALRUSES

But are good jumpers.

BELUGA WHALES

We can jump over the .

WALRUSES

Whee!

Great 🦭 jumping!

WALRUS

We made it to the .

ISLAND

Look how all of the  has

ICE

melted.

Don't worry, baby .

POLAR BEARS

We will take you to your mommy, where there is a lot of ICE and SNOW.

Do you know how?

A  ! Yes!

HELICOPTER

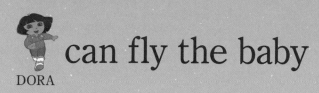 

 can fly the baby POLAR BEARS

back to their mommy in her

HELICOPTER !

Hooray! We did it!

Thank you for helping us

save the  !

POLAR BEARS

Rescue complete!